# gigi

# God's Little Princess®
## Treasury

This book belongs to:

Princess _____

Library of Congress Cataloging-in-Publication Data

Walsh, Sheila, 1956–
 God's little princess treasury / by Sheila Walsh ; illustrated by Meredith Johnson.
  v. cm. — (Gigi)
 Summary: A collection of four previously-published stories about Gigi and her friends,
who discover that they are God's little princesses, then try to live accordingly.
 Contents: Gigi, God's little princess—Royal tea party—The pink ballerina—The Purple Ponies.
 ISBN 978-1-4003-1472-0 (hardcover)
 [1. Christian life—Fiction. 2. Princesses—Fiction. 3. Friendship—Fiction.] I. Johnson, Meredith, ill. II. Title.
 PZ7.W16894God 2009
 [E] —dc22

                                                        2009015563

Printed in China
15 16 17 DSC 6 5 4

Mfg:DSC
Shenzhen, China
July 2015-PPO#9354520

# gigi
# God's Little Princess®
# Treasury

By Sheila Walsh
Illustrated by Meredith Johnson

THOMAS NELSON
*Since 1798*

NASHVILLE   MEXICO CITY   RIO DE JANEIRO

# Contents

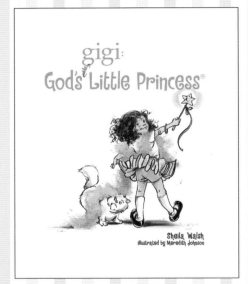
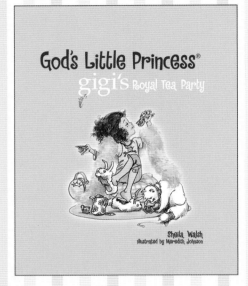

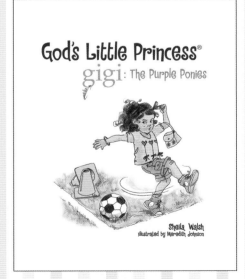

# gigi:
# God's Little Princess®

# gigi:
# God's Little Princess®

## By Sheila Walsh
### Illustrated by Meredith Johnson

This book
is dedicated
to all God's
little princesses.

Gigi was a princess. She had known it from birth.

*The Father has loved us so much . . . that we are called children of God.*
*1 John 3:1*

Every night when her daddy kissed her forehead, he would say, "Good night, princess. Sweet dreams!"

At times Gigi wondered why they didn't live in a castle and where *were* the royal jewels?

She assumed they were locked away in a vault somewhere for safekeeping, and when she was all grown up or ten—whichever came first—they would be presented to her.

One thing troubled Gigi. She didn't exactly look like a traditional princess.

No matter how hard she scrubbed, she could not get rid of the freckles on her nose.

No matter how hard
she brushed her hair,
she could not get it to
lie down and behave.

"I *so* need a crown to flatten this," she thought.

15

Gigi's best friend was Frances. Frances was not royal, but Gigi loved her anyway.

"One must bond with one's subjects," she told Frances.

"Thank you, Your Highness," Frances replied
with appropriate gratitude.

Gigi loved to discover things. She assumed that
her royal ancestors had left treasures for her,
and she was determined to find each one.

So far she had uncovered four buttons, two pieces of velvet ribbon, and a jar that may once have been a glass slipper. Her future looked promising.

Gigi was sure that one day she would rule over many subjects who would bow when she entered a room.

She practiced on her cat.

The cat seemed reluctant to cooperate.

"This attitude must change if you expect to be great in my kingdom," she told Lord Fluffy.

Her favorite thing to do was to have a tea party in the backyard (or the "outer court," as she called it) with Frances.

"May I ask a question, Your Royal Highness?" Frances asked one day.

"Speak," Gigi replied.

"What makes you a princess, and why am I not a princess?"

"Isn't it obvious?" Gigi asked.

"Not immediately," Frances replied.

"Hmm," said Gigi.

That night Gigi asked her father,
"Daddy, what makes me a princess?"

"You have always been a princess," he said.

"Yes, but where are the royal jewels and
where is my crown and when do I begin my
reign?" she asked. "I think I'm ready."

Her father laughed. "I think you are ready to
go to sleep, young lady. Good night, princess.
Sweet dreams."

The next morning, Gigi decided to clear up the matter with her mom.

"Mommy, Frances asked me what makes me a princess and why is she not a princess."

"You are both princesses," her mom replied.

Gigi was shocked by this revelation!

She sat on her bed with Lord Fluffy.

"Should I be the one to tell Frances?
Will I have to share my jewels?
Will she have her own jewels?
How will the land be divided?
To whom will Lord Fluffy bow first?"

"May I please call Frances?" she asked her mom.

"Yes, you may. You can use the kitchen phone if you like."

"This is royal business, Mom. I will need to use the pink phone," Gigi replied.

"Frances, are you sitting down?" she asked.

"No, but I can," Frances said.

"I think it would be wise," Gigi suggested.

"Frances, . . . I have shocking royal news: you are a princess too!"

Frances thought she might faint, but the moment passed.

"How do you know?" she asked. "And why has my family been keeping this from me? Does this mean that my daddy is a king?"

This thought had never occurred to Gigi. Life was becoming very confusing. She was now surrounded by royalty.

That night she asked, "Daddy, are you a king?"

"Why would you think that?" he said.

"If I am a princess, you must be a king."

"Well, you are a daughter of a very great King," Daddy said. "He is King above any other king."

Big tears began to pool in the corners of Gigi's eyes. "Are you not my daddy?" she asked.

"Of course I am," Daddy said, squeezing her tightly. "But we are children of the greatest King of all. This King rules over everything there is, and you are His daughter. You are God's little princess! Now it's time to get to sleep. Good night, Gigi. Sweet dreams."

"Good night, Daddy."

*Everyone who believes that Jesus is the Christ is God's child.*
*1 John 5:1*

Gigi snuggled into bed with her royal pink phone on the pillow beside her. "Just wait till I tell Frances my news tomorrow, Lord Fluffy! She's sure to faint this time."

"I wonder," Gigi said, patting her unruly hair, "just exactly when will I get my crown?"

The princess is very beautiful. Her gown is woven with gold. In her beautiful clothes she is brought to the king.

Psalm 45:13–14

# gigi's Royal Tea Party

# God's Little Princess®
## gigi's Royal Tea Party

By Sheila Walsh

Illustrated by Meredith Johnson

This book is dedicated to all of God's Little Princesses. Being loving and kind is more important than getting everything right!

Gigi had big news.

She sat on the bed with her cat discussing her problem.
"Lord Fluffy, it is my royal duty as princess to tell Frances the
good news," she said. "How shall I make my announcement?"

Lord Fluffy seemed more concerned with Gigi's bunny slippers than with her exciting news.

"Certainly not!" she cried indignantly. "One does not pounce on a princess with this kind of news. It has to be delivered . . . very carefully. I am sure Frances will faint this time."

"Daddy, if you had to deliver wonderful but very important news and there wasn't a moment to spare, how would you do it?" Gigi asked the next morning at breakfast.

"I think I would pick up the phone, princess, if the news was urgent," he said.

44

"Hmm, I was trying to find something more . . . royal,"
Gigi said.

*Let the teaching of Christ live in you richly. Use all wisdom to teach and strengthen each other. . . .*

*Colossians 3:16*

Gigi lay on her bed and tried to think of ways a princess could make a royal announcement. "I've got it! I could have a band. There must be a procession!"

She picked up her pink telephone and began to dial.

"Maggie, this is Gigi," she said. "I need you to play for a royal announcement tomorrow. How would you like to be a part of Gigi's Pink Parade Players?"

"Sorry, Gigi, but I have dance class tomorrow," her friend replied.

"But this is important!" Gigi said. "And one would consider it an honor just to be asked!"

"Sorry," Maggie replied. "But if you want, you can borrow my flute."

"Do you think I could learn to play in one night?" Gigi asked.

"Well, perhaps not."

Gigi tried all her friends, but it was no use. The answer was always the same. "Sorry, but . . .

"My dog ate my drum!"

"I broke my pinkie finger."

"My brother sat on my trumpet."

"My lizard is loose!"

Suddenly it came to her. "I shall simply have to hire a band."
Gigi took her pink piggy bank off the shelf and emptied out
the contents.

"I don't think this will be enough," she said. "I think I would
need at least five dollars."

"I know!" Gigi said jumping up and down on her bed. "I could make my announcement on TV."

Gigi imagined herself standing in front of the camera:
"Hello, America, this is Princess Gigi interrupting your regularly scheduled program with an important announcement! Frances is God's little princess too!"

"Too dangerous," Gigi decided, "Frances would definitely faint."

"A small plane—that's what we need, Lord Fluffy! We could fly low over Frances' house with a humongous sign."

"No, too predictable," she said.

"Now I've really got it!" she cried so loudly that Lord Fluffy shot up in the air. "We will have a royal tea party. That is the proper way."

"And Frances will love it."

Gigi ran downstairs to ask Mommy.

"Mommy, may I invite Frances for a royal tea party tomorrow?"

"I think that would be lovely," her mommy replied. "Is it a special occasion?"

"The most special of all," Gigi said. "Tomorrow I will tell Frances that she is a princess too. What joy!"

Gigi started preparing right away. "Mommy, do you know where the balloons are?" she asked.

"They're in a big box in the playroom, Gigi," Mommy said. "How many do you need?"

"I need a lot . . . and I can only use pink ones for the royal cat-drawn carriage," Gigi replied.

"What's the cat-drawn carriage for?" Mommy asked.

"I feel that I should deliver the invitation in person," Gigi replied.

Gigi sat on the floor and blew—

and blew         and blew         and blew.

Soon Gigi had six pink balloons but was feeling . . . not-so-in-the-pink.

Gigi and Lord Fluffy set off as Mommy watched from the porch. "Oh! Mommy, will you call Frances and ask her to look out of her window?" Gigi asked.

"Tail up, Lord Fluffy! You should be thrilled to be part of the royal announcement parade."

As they approached Frances' house, Lord Fluffy jumped out and ran away, balloons dragging. Gigi was horrified.

She looked up at Frances' bedroom window. "I'm going home! *Everything* has gone wrong!"

"This has been one of the worst days in my whole life!" Gigi announced to Mommy. "I quit!" she added. "Frances will just have to live in ignorance of the extremely large hugeness of what I had to share."

"Do you think Frances would quit on you, Gigi?" Mommy asked gently. "Or do you think that God would quit on us if we didn't understand at first how much He loves us?"

"No, Mommy, I'm sure God would never quit on His little princesses."

When Gigi came downstairs in her p.j.'s, Daddy was laughing.

"What's so funny, Daddy?" she asked.

"I just got off the phone with Frances' father. He wants to
know if she can stop looking out of the window now!"

"She was still looking?" Gigi asked with a smile.
"She really is a very good friend! Perhaps I should
just call her and invite her to the tea party after all."

The next day, the two friends sat out in the yard talking.
Soon Mommy brought out the tea tray.

"Thank you, Mommy," Gigi said.

"Yes, thank you," Frances added. "Gigi, what were you going
to show me yesterday?"

"I looked out of the window for hours, but the only thing I saw was your cat running through the yard with balloons!"

Gigi sighed with embarrassment. "Let's just ask the blessing."

"Dear God, thank You for my friend Frances
and for the wonderful news that I have been
trying to tell her for days . . . that she is
Your daughter and God's little princess just like
me, but it's been very hard and things kept going
wrong and I almost quit, but Frances didn't quit
on me and You don't quit on us, so I am here once
more to announce to Frances that she is Your
princess too, and I'm going to let her use the royal
cup so now she knows and . . . and . . . and . . .
Amen!"

*Before the world was made, God decided to make us his own children
through Jesus Christ.*

*Ephesians 1:5*

Gigi opened her eyes and smiled. Things had gone even better than expected. As she moved the royal cup to Frances' side of the table, she gazed down at her best friend lying flat on the grass.

Frances had fainted!

Gigi knelt beside her dazed friend and said, "This is the best day of our lives, Frances. We are both God's little princesses!"

God chose you out of all the people on Earth
as his cherished personal treasure.

Deuteronomy 14:2 (MESSAGE)

# gigi: The Pink Ballerina

This book is
dedicated to every
Little Princess who has
ever fallen off her shoes
or tripped over her
feather boa!

# God's Little Princess®
## gigi: The Pink Ballerina

By Sheila Walsh
Illustrated by Meredith Johnson

# "Bye, Frances,"

Gigi called to her best friend after church.

"I'll talk to you later. I have a lot of royal thinking to do!"

"Royal thinking!" her daddy said as they drove home. "That sounds important."

"It is very important, Daddy," Gigi replied. "It *is* a royal command and it's in the Bible and it was our memory verse today and it applies particularly to princesses!"

"My goodness, take a breath, Gigi," her daddy said with a smile.

"What is your verse, Gigi?" her mommy asked.

"It's from the Psssssalmps."

"Oh, I love the Psalms," her daddy said. "Do you know the verse by heart yet?"

"Well . . . kind of," Gigi answered as she pulled her lesson sheet out of her pocket. "It was something to do with dancing."

"What happened here?" her mommy asked.

"Well," Gigi began, "Will, who is usually not very nice to me but was nice to me today, gave me a piece of gum. I thought it would be ungodly not to take it."

"Ungodly?" her daddy asked, trying to stifle his laughter.

"Yes, but then the teacher said we were going to pray, and I thought it might be more ungodly to pray with gum in my mouth. So I tore a piece off my lesson sheet and spit my gum out and . . ."

"Oh no! This is a royal disaster!" Gigi gasped.
"I only have half the verse."

"Don't worry, Gigi," her daddy said.
"I'll find the other half for you later."

Gigi spent the rest of the day doing royal thinking.
She kept repeating the line on the paper. "I wonder
what it means?"

*Let them praise his name in dance . . .*

"Oh my goodness!" she squealed.
"I've got it!"

Startled, Tiara ran around the room barking.

Lord Fluffy opened one eye, muttered
something in cat language, and went
back to sleep.

"I will have to call Frances at once!" Gigi said.

"Tiara, do be quiet. This is official princess business."

"Frances, I have completed my royal thinking," Gigi began.

"You have?" Frances said, not particularly surprised.

"Yes, I have," Gigi continued. "Are you sitting down?"

"I am," Frances assured her. "I always do when you call . . . just in case."

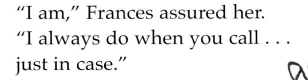

"Frances, what do you get if you put two princesses together with a dance?" Gigi asked.

"A very small dance?" Frances suggested.

"No, no," Gigi said, rising to her full height. "You get . . . BALLET! Come over tomorrow, and we'll practice."

"Listen up, everyone," Gigi said the next day, tapping the end of her bed with a wooden spoon. "We will begin by warming up. Stretch your arms up over your head like this."

Frances and Tiara seemed willing to oblige. But Lord Fluffy was reluctant, deciding instead to pounce on Tiara's tail.

"Do you feel warm yet?" Gigi asked.

"I do," Frances replied. "Now what?"

Just then, Gigi's mommy looked in the door.
"Hmm, I think you two could use some help," she said.
"What about a ballet class?"

"What a royal idea!" Gigi said as the princess ballerinas
collapsed onto the bed.

A few days later on their way to ballet class, Gigi asked, "How many girls will be in our class?"

"I'm not sure, Gigi," her mommy said. "Miss Chambord said that it's a class for beginners."

"Well, we probably won't be in that one for long," Gigi said. "Frances and I have ballet in our blood, don't we, Frances?"

"In our blood!" Frances repeated with flair.

"Welcome, *la petites*!" Miss Chambord said.
"We will begin by working on our poise."

"Did she say, 'Working on our noise'?"
Gigi asked.

"Poise, not noise," Frances whispered.

Miss Chambord smiled. "Poise is the way you stand.
Like so." She raised her right arm above her head.

"Now, bend your knees
and rise onto your tippytoes.
Try to be elegant like the
swan. Long necks, long necks!"

"This is killing me!" Gigi said to Frances.

And it didn't get any easier. . . .

*"Bien, la petites!* Now we move into the *plié*—but graceful, girls, with grace!"

"Did she ask us to say grace?" Gigi asked.

Frances rolled her eyes.

"Now, girls," Miss Chambord said, "form a circle, and we will dance around like the little butterfly."

Everything was going very well until the girl behind
Gigi stepped on the end of Gigi's feather boa.

The girls all went down like dominoes.

That night, Gigi sat on her bed. "I can't be a princess, Daddy. I just can't do it," Gigi said with big tears rolling down her cheeks.

"What do you mean, Gigi?" her daddy asked. "Of course you are a princess!"

"God won't let me be one of His princesses," Gigi cried. "I tried to dance, but I tripped everyone up with my royal pink boa! I wanted to do it perfectly and make Him proud of me."

Daddy smiled. "Gigi, you are God's little princess because He chose you, not because of anything you do or how well you do it. He looks at your heart. You can show Him that you love Him in lots of ways."

Her daddy looked around the room.
"Where is your favorite royal boa?"

"I gave it to the girl who stepped on it. She was crying
because she thought it was her fault—but it wasn't
really—and I wanted to make her feel better. So I
gave her the boa, and it made her smile."

"That was a kind thing to do, Gigi," her daddy said. "It makes God happy when you show kindness to others. And I think we can find you another pink feathered boa. Good night, princess."

"Good night, Daddy," Gigi said, stifling a big yawn.

Gigi lay quietly with Tiara on her tummy and Lord Fluffy on her pillow. Her daddy stepped back into her room.

"I found the rest of your verse," he said. "It's 'Let them praise his name in dance; strike up the band and make great music!'"

Suddenly, Gigi sat straight up. "That's it! We'll form a band. Just wait till Frances hears about this!"

Let them praise his name in dance; strike up
the band and make great music!

Psalm 149:3 (MESSAGE)

# gigi: The Purple Ponies

This book is
dedicated to all God's
princesses—the ones who
can kick the ball and the
ones who have a ball
cheering them on!

# God's Little Princess®
## gigi: The Purple Ponies

By Sheila Walsh
Illustrated by Meredith Johnson

Gigi was not a boring princess.

She *did* like to dress up and was completely committed to pink, but she also loved trying new things! Today, Gigi turned her royal attention to soccer.

"Frances," Gigi said, attempting unsuccessfully to keep a soccer ball in the air, "today could change our lives forever!"

"Wow!" Frances replied with appropriate awe. "Forever is a *very* long time."

Gigi looked around. "It feels like it is taking forever to get through this line. There must be forty-two bazillion girls here!"

"Daddy, I am ready to get going. I am bursting with readiness. I have so much readiness it's coming out my ears!" Gigi said, bouncing up and down.

Gigi's daddy smiled. "Soccer is a very popular sport for princesses."

"But I am a natural athlete," Gigi replied.

"She's very good," Frances agreed. "Today she kicked her p.j.'s across the bedroom, and they landed right on Lord Fluffy's head."

"That is impressive!" Daddy agreed.

Finally, all the girls in front of them had signed in and received a nametag.

"Do you have any pink ones?" Gigi asked.

"We are the '*Purple* Ponies,'" the lady behind the sign-up desk replied. "We don't wear pink."

"That is tragic," Gigi whispered to Frances.

"Hello and welcome, girls. I'm Coach Prescott. Today, I will be picking fourteen girls to play with the Purple Ponies—seven for the first team and seven reserves. That means, unfortunately, that not everyone will be able to play on the soccer team this season."

"Poor things," Gigi whispered to Frances. "When we are chosen, we can look happy but not too happy. It wouldn't be nice for the poor girls who don't make the team."

"Girls," Coach Prescott began, "when I blow the whistle, take a ball and dribble it up to the line and back. Be in control of the ball at all times."

Gigi laughed so loudly that everyone turned to stare.

"Do you have something funny you would like to share with us all . . . Gigi?" Coach said, reading Gigi's nametag.

"No, ma'am," Gigi replied. "I do sincerely apologize for my not-so-royal behavior. It's . . . just that I've never been asked to drool on a ball before."

"That's not quite what I meant," Coach said with a smile. "Samantha Parker, will you please show all the new girls how to dribble a ball?"

"Oh . . . my . . . goodness!" Frances said to Gigi as they watched the team's star athlete control the ball.

"She is good," Gigi agreed. "I hope I don't make her feel bad when I show my stuff."

"Well, don't hold back, Gigi," Frances said.

"I couldn't, Frances," Gigi said with quiet dignity.
"It's just not in me."

Finally, it was their time to shine. The coach blew the whistle. Girls began to slowly dribble the ball toward the line.

But Gigi's first kick sent
her ball soaring across the field.

The next time, she accidentally
kicked it behind her.

On her third try, she tripped
and fell on top of the ball.

"My ball stinks!" Gigi said in frustration,
sprawled on the grass.

"It did seem a little . . . loose," Frances agreed.

"You were very good, Frances," Gigi said.

"Thank you, Gigi," Frances replied. "I had a friendly ball."

"Daddy, did you see my ball?" Gigi asked while they waited to see who would be on the team. "It was faulty. . . or it had a mouse inside it . . . or a magnet that was mysteriously being controlled from outer space," she suggested.

"Gigi," her daddy said, "it may be that soccer is just not for you."

Big tears began to roll down Gigi's cheeks.

"God has given you lots of gifts," her daddy explained. "It's your job to find out what those gifts are and use them to shine like God's princess."

# "Gigi! Look!"

Frances shouted.

"Coach has posted the list."

120

Frances took off at breakneck speed as Gigi's daddy dried Gigi's eyes.

By the time Gigi reached Frances, she was heading back off the field.

"Well?" Gigi asked. "Are we Ponies? Are we Purple Ponies?"

"Not this time, Gigi," Frances said.

"Congratulations, Frances,"
Gigi's daddy said.

"Well, excuse me, Daddy," Gigi said.
"But you don't usually congratulate
someone for gross failuredom."

"What do you mean, Gigi?" Daddy said.
"Frances made it onto the team. Didn't
she tell you?"

Gigi stared at Frances. "I don't understand," she said.

"Gigi," Frances began, "when I saw my name and not your name on the list, I didn't know what to say. It wouldn't be as much fun without my very best friend."

"Well, Frances," Gigi said, "if God has made you good at soccer, you should use your gift. He might get cross if you're not out there shining!"

"But we wanted to be on the team together, Gigi," Frances said.

"I'm sure there's an answer to this problem, Frances,"
Gigi promised. "I just need to do some royal thinking
about it."

First, they took Frances home. Then . . .

"Daddy, I've got it!" announced Gigi as Lord Fluffy
and Tiara welcomed them home. "I've figured out how
both Frances and I can be Purple Ponies. Listen to this:

Go, Ponies—Purple, Purple Ponies!
Kick the ball and show them all.
Go, Ponies, go!

"I'll be at Frances' games as a Purple Ponies cheerleader.
After all . . . I am very loud, so that must be one of my gifts!"

We all have different gifts.
Each gift came because of the
grace that God gave us.
Romans 12:6